W9-BOB-957

# BREAKOUT

By Tracey West

SCHOLASTIC INC.

If you purchased this book without a cover, you should be aware that this book is stolen property. It was reported as "unsold and destroyed" to the publisher, and neither the author nor the publisher has received any payment for this "stripped book."

LEGO, the LEGO logo, NINJAGO, the Brick and Knob configurations and the Minifigure are trademarks of the LEGO Group. © 2015 the LEGO Group. Produced by Scholastic Inc. under license from the LEGO Group.

All rights reserved. Published by Scholastic Inc., *Publishers since 1920.* SCHOLASTIC and associated logos are trademarks and/or registered trademarks of Scholastic Inc.

No part of this publication may be reproduced, stored in a retrieval system, or transmitted in any form or by any means, electronic, mechanical, photocopying, recording, or otherwise, without written permission of the publisher. For information regarding permission, write to Scholastic Inc., Attention: Permissions Department, 557 Broadway, New York, NY 10012.

This book is a work of fiction. Names, characters, places, and incidents are either the product of the author's imagination or are used fictitiously, and any resemblance to actual persons, living or dead, business establishments, events, or locales is entirely coincidental.

ISBN 978-0-545-82551-1

10 9 8 7 6 5 4 3 2 1          15 16 17 18 19/0

Printed in the U.S.A.                           40
First printing 2015

Book design by Rick DeMonico

# ANGEL PARK

## SoccerStars

### 3

# VICTORY GOAL

# By Dean Hughes

### Illustrated by Dennis Lyall

**Bullseye Books • Alfred A. Knopf**
*New York*

A BULLSEYE BOOK PUBLISHED BY ALFRED A. KNOPF, INC.
Copyright © 1992 by Dean Hughes
Cover art copyright © 1992 by Steve Brennan
Interior illustrations copyright © 1992 by Dennis Lyall
ANGEL PARK ALL-STARS characters copyright © 1989
by Alfred A. Knopf, Inc.
ANGEL PARK SOCCER STARS characters copyright © 1991
by Alfred A. Knopf, Inc.

All rights reserved under International and Pan-American Copyright
Conventions. Published in the United States by Alfred A. Knopf, Inc.,
New York, and simultaneously in Canada by Random House of Canada
Limited, Toronto. Distributed by Random House, Inc., New York.

Library of Congress Cataloging-in-Publication Data
Hughes, Dean, 1943–
Victory goal / by Dean Hughes ; illustrated by Dennis Lyall.
p.    cm. — (Angel Park soccer stars ; 3)
Summary: Sterling Malone is a fullback who wants to be a forward,
just like his big brother.
ISBN 0-679-82637-8 (pbk.) — ISBN 0-679-92637-2 (lib. bdg.)
[1. Soccer—Fiction.]  I. Lyall, Dennis, ill.  II. Title.
III. Series: Hughes, Dean, 1943– Angel Park soccer stars ; 3.
PZ7.H87312Vi   1992   [Fic]—dc20   91-23321
RL: 2.7
First Bullseye Books edition: March 1992

Manufactured in the United States of America
10  9  8  7  6  5  4  3  2  1

*for Clayton Harrison and Nathan Keith*

# ★1★

## So Close!

Sterling Malone saw Klaus Vandegraff, the Kickers' star forward, take the pass. Klaus had broken free from his defender and was charging toward the goal. Sterling left his own man and cut toward Klaus.

But Klaus stopped, pulled the ball back, and let Sterling slide by, and then he dropped the ball off to his brother, Peter, who was also running toward the goal. Sterling was supposed to be covering Peter, and now Peter was all alone.

Peter took the ball in full stride. Nate Matheson, goalie for the Angel Park Pride, had no choice but to come up to meet him.

And he did a good job of cutting off Peter's shooting angle.

But that's when Klaus slipped past Sterling and took a return pass. Klaus *banged* the ball into the net.

And the score was tied, 3 to 3.

The Pride had played a great game. They had led all the way. And they had been only four minutes away from a big victory in their first game of the regular season. But now they would have to start all over again.

Sterling was furious with himself. He bent over and put his hands on his knees. His legs were wet with sweat. His heart was pounding, and he was struggling to catch his breath.

Sterling had given everything he had today, but now he had really blown it. The most basic rule of defense was never to get split between two attackers.

Sterling felt a hand on his shoulder, and he looked up. Nate said, "You had no choice, Sterling. When Klaus got by Jared, you had to gamble."

"I know. But I got caught between Klaus and Peter, and Klaus got away from me. I should have let someone else get Peter."

"That happens to everybody. Don't worry about it."

And then Jacob Scott yelled, "That's okay. We'll just get our attack going. We've been too careful. Let's go get a goal and win this thing."

Heidi Wells yelled, "That's right. Let's go after 'em."

The team began to pick up the spirit, and Sterling found himself hoping that somehow the Pride could still win, so he wouldn't have to feel that he had lost the game.

But then he looked off toward the side of the field. His dad and his older brother, Reggie, were standing together. Reggie yelled, "Don't worry about it. Just get that goal back. Score one yourself."

That meant that Reggie thought the goal was Sterling's fault. And of course, he would know. He was 4 years older than Sterling. *And* he was a great soccer player himself. In fact, Reggie's biggest problem was that he was so good at so many sports he had trouble choosing which ones to play.

But Reggie was no fullback—no defensive specialist. He played forward, and he was the leading scorer on his team every year. Sterling didn't like to admit it, but he was jealous of that.

Sterling got ready for the kickoff. He tried to put his mistake out of his mind and concentrate on playing hard defense. The Pride couldn't let the Kickers get another goal.

Clayton Lindsay, the Pride's star midfielder, turned around and shouted to the fullbacks, "Let's go! When we get the ball, let's *all* take it upfield. We need to keep the pressure on, and we need to score!"

Sterling didn't say anything. He never did a lot of yelling. But he knew what he wanted to do. He wanted to make up for his mistake. Fullbacks didn't score very often, but they could do it if the team brought everyone into the attack. The coach called that "total soccer."

More than anything, with his brother and his dad watching, Sterling wanted to prove that he could play this game.

But the ball was soon moving toward his end of the field, and that meant defense, not attack. Patty Pinelli, the Kickers' left wing, slid toward the middle of the field and then looped a lead pass to the right wing, who volleyed the ball across to Peter Van-degraff.

Sterling marked him close.

Peter faked right and broke left, but Sterling stayed square with his shoulders and kept his feet moving. He reacted quickly, and Peter couldn't get past him.

And then, when Peter tried to pass off, he let the ball get too far out in front, and Sterling saw his chance. He blocked Peter with his shoulder, reached in with his left foot, and knocked the ball away.

He was after the ball just as quickly, and he controlled it with his right foot. By then, Peter had turned defender, and he blocked Sterling's chance to move upfield. But Peter was a better attacker than defender, and when Sterling faked, Peter lost his balance. Sterling darted past him.

Sterling had room, and he drove hard, dribbling the ball into the midfield. When a defender closed in, he saw the guy coming, and he kicked a quick pass to Clayton. Clayton took a couple of slow steps with the ball and then burst past his defender.

Clayton broke free into the forward part

of the field. He ran hard, dribbling. Sterling ran with him, just off to Clayton's left. When two defenders doubled on him, Clayton managed to split them and then flip the ball back to Sterling.

And now Sterling was free. He had a great angle to the goal.

He rushed at the goalie until the guy made his move toward him. And then Sterling lifted a looping shot over the goalie's head.

It was a perfect shot.

Almost.

It was just a *little* long. Instead of dropping in front of the goal and bouncing into the net, it struck the crossbar and bounced over the goal.

Sterling had already shot his arms up in the air in triumph. But then he sunk to the ground as he saw the narrow miss.

"Nice shot!" Henry White yelled from behind Sterling. "Man, you almost had it. It was *soooooo* close."

"Close doesn't count!" Sterling said, and he got up.

Then, as he turned to jog down the field to get back to his position, Clayton said, "One more pass, and we would have had it, Sterling. You didn't have to take it in all the way by yourself."

"Hey, he had a good shot," Jacob said. "He almost made it."

"Yeah, but he had to lift the ball over the goalie's head. And that's tough," Clayton answered. "Heidi was breaking in from the left. She would have had an easy shot. A good soccer player has to see those things."

Sterling tried not to let Clayton bother him. The guy always had something to say, no matter what happened.

But Sterling knew something else. Clayton *did* have a better vision of the field. He probably would have made the pass—or scored. That's why Sterling played defense. He was big, and he was quick, but he didn't have the vision or the ball-handling skills that Clayton had. Or, at least, that's what Sterling thought.

As Sterling ran down the field, he didn't look to the sidelines, but he heard his brother yell, "Great shot, Sterling! You *almost* got it."

Almost. That was the difference between

Sterling and Reggie when it came to soccer. Reggie made the goals, and Sterling *almost* made them.

But the game wasn't over. Sterling might have another chance yet. He still wanted to win this game.

"All right, fullbacks," Nate was yelling from the goal, "we gotta play defense. We can't give up another goal, no matter what."

And Sterling knew that was true. Overtime, or even a tie, was better than blowing the game. He knew he really should be thinking about shutting the Kickers down. That was a fullback's main job.

"Wall them off!" Tammy Hill was yelling. "Pack in and cover everybody."

The Kickers were working the ball forward, and the Pride midfielders were making them work. Lian Jie was all over the Kickers' midfielder, who was trying to find someone to take a pass.

Jared yelled, "Way to cover, Lian! Way to go!" And then he shouted to Sterling, "Don't give Peter an *inch* of room this time."

Sterling moved in close on Peter. He knew Jared was right. But he wanted that ball again. He wanted to get off one more shot, and this time he wanted to *make* it.

Klaus took a pass from the wing and dribbled across the field. Sterling watched his eyes and knew that Klaus wanted to get the ball to Peter. But Sterling was tight on his man, and Klaus had to look for someone else.

That's when Clayton saw his chance to leave his man and double on Klaus. He picked Klaus clean, and *bang,* Clayton was gone with the ball.

Sterling ran up the field too. He watched from a distance as Jacob took a pass. But Jacob let a defender sneak in from his blind side and strip the ball.

The Kickers were coming at him again, and Sterling told himself to get back and cover Peter.

Time was running out. Sterling was afraid he had had his one big chance to score. And it had ended up as a big *almost.*

# ★2★

# Kicked

Now that the Kickers were back on attack, they were pulling out all the stops. A quick midfielder tried to dribble past Clayton. The midfielder set his foot to cut. But then he let out a little scream and crumpled to the ground.

And he didn't get up.

Clayton took over the ball, but the referee blew his whistle to call time-out.

The boy had twisted his knee, and he was lying on the ground holding on to it. Sterling felt sorry for the kid. He seemed to be in real pain. Sterling walked over to him, along with a lot of other players, to get a closer look.

The Kickers' coaches came on to the field and bent over the boy. They were still talking to him and checking his knee when Sterling saw Reggie hurrying down the touchline.

"Sterling, come here," Reggie called.

Sterling walked over to the side of the field, and Reggie came up close. He spoke quietly but intensely. "I just checked. There's less than three minutes to go in the match. You guys are shutting them off, all right, but you've got to get your attack going."

"I know," Sterling said, "but I have to be careful. I already messed up once. I don't want to give up another goal. Not now, especially."

"Sure. That's right. But when you get your chance, you have to overload their defense. Your attack is twice as good when someone with your speed gets up there in the goal area with the forwards."

Sterling liked hearing that. It was what he wanted to believe. But he also knew what Coach Toscano always told the fullbacks: Above all else, they should never let anyone get between them and the goal.

"I have to be careful, Reggie," Sterling said. "I can't let myself get beat again."

"Hey, you don't win games by being careful. You have to be aggressive."

The coaches were helping the Kickers' midfielder off the field. The kid was putting weight on his leg. Maybe the injury wasn't as bad as it had seemed at first.

Sterling told himself that Reggie was right. If he could help get a goal, he was going to feel a whole lot better about this match.

But after the restart, another minute went by, and the two teams kept trading steals in the middle of the field. Time was running out.

Sterling found himself edging forward, watching for a chance to break upfield with his team the instant it went on attack.

One time Angel Park did take over the ball, and Sterling made his break. But the Kickers' right wing slipped in and took the ball back. Sterling had to recover quickly and get back between Peter and the goal.

As the Kickers came up the field on attack, Sterling got ready. But he was thinking attack. He wanted to get that ball and *go*.

And he got his chance.

Peter Vandegraff ran toward his own midfielder to take a pass. Sterling darted after the ball too, and he won the race. He reached for the ball first, but he was going too fast. As he tried to control the ball, it took a high bounce.

Sterling tried to get his foot on the ball, but he slid past. As he tried to catch his balance, he fell to one knee.

That was the break Peter needed. He kicked the ball past Sterling and then ran after it. Sterling was up quickly and charging after Peter, but Peter saw Klaus angling toward the goal, and he lofted a long pass to the center of the field.

Klaus leaped for the ball and headed it to Patty Pinelli, who had gotten clear. Jared covered her, but Peter was sprinting down the field with Sterling a step behind him. Patty flipped the ball back to Peter. He controlled the pass and charged toward the goal.

Sterling was beat, and Peter was going to have a great shot. Nate left the goal and broke to his left, but he was too late to cut Peter off.

Sterling was out of position, but he tried to come from behind Peter and stab at the ball.

He almost pulled it off.

His foot did hit the ball and knock it away. But at the same time, he hit Peter's leg and knocked him flat.

Sterling didn't have to hear the whistle. He didn't have to hear the referee call for a penalty shot. He already knew he had tripped Peter in the goal area.

And he knew one more thing. Peter didn't miss penalty shots.

"What were you *doing?*" Clayton yelled at Sterling.

Before he could say more, Coach Toscano shouted from the sidelines, "That's enough, Clayton."

Still, Sterling knew Clayton was right. He had blown it—again.

The referee set the ball at the penalty spot. Nate got ready in the goal.

Peter hunched forward and looked at the ball. He took a deep breath.

Everyone waited.

The players on the field were silent.

But along the sidelines the fans and substitute players were all yelling.

Sterling didn't know what there was to yell about. Most players could make penalty shots. The goalie had to take on the shot from close range. Unless the shooter made a big mistake, the goalie didn't have a chance.

And Peter was deadly. He had grown up playing in Holland, and a soccer ball was a part of him. He could do anything with it.

Peter jogged forward.

Sterling turned his back. He couldn't stand to watch.

He heard Peter's foot smack the ball cleanly. And then he heard the Kickers' players and fans go crazy.

When Sterling glanced back, the Kickers were all jumping on Peter, and Nate was still lying on the ground, with his face in the grass.

That told the whole story.

The Pride had a minute left, but that was not much to work with. They did make a great effort. The team went all out on attack, and the fullbacks pushed forward in the hope of overpowering the defense.

But the Kickers packed in on defense, and they cut off every chance for a shot.

Sterling tried his best—as did everyone else—but the seconds ticked away, *fast,* and suddenly it was all over.

The Pride had lost.

Angel Park had come very close to beating one of the best teams in the league. A win would have been a great start to the season. But now they were 0 and 1, and a good start had turned into a disaster.

Or at least that's how it seemed to Sterling.

Coach Toscano didn't agree. He called the team over, and he told them, "Kids, I'm really proud of you. We played the best soccer we've ever played. I know you feel bad. But I can promise you if you keep playing like this, you're going to win a lot of matches."

"We *had* them," Chris Baca said, "and we let them get away."

"Well, yes. That's true in a way," the coach said. "But give the Kickers some credit. They have great talent, and they play hard. One little mistake, and they make a team pay for it. The next time we play them, we just have to cut down on some of those mistakes."

Sterling knew who had made the worst mistakes—the ones that had turned the game around.

He looked down at the grass and tried to fight back the tears. He kept saying to himself, "You lost the game. You lost the game."

"So what about it?" Coach Toscano asked the players. "Wasn't that fun?"

No one answered.

"Sure it was," the coach told them. "This is a great game, and it's fun to play. You can't win all the time, and you have to enjoy the good competition even if you lose. That was a *great* match."

Sterling couldn't see that. He got up and walked away.

And that's when he heard Clayton say, "I don't know what Sterling was thinking about today. If he hadn't let Peter get behind him, he wouldn't have had to trip the guy."

Clayton didn't say it to Sterling. But he said it plenty loud enough for him to hear. And that was no accident.

Sterling just kept walking. He knew Clayton was right. Besides, tears were running down his cheeks. He didn't want anyone to see that.

He wiped the tears on his sleeve. It would be bad enough if the players saw him crying, but it would be even worse if his brother saw him.

# In Sterling's Room

Sterling didn't say much on the way home from the game. His dad told him he had played very well. Reggie even took some of the blame for what happened. "Maybe I should have kept my mouth shut. If I hadn't said anything, you probably wouldn't have gotten out of position."

In a way, that was true. But it didn't help.

Reggie could have pulled it off. He would have known when to get back, and he would have done it somehow. Reggie did everything right. It was like he had an extra sense. Every team he played for turned out to be a winner.

He was also a great student. Teachers

always told Sterling on the first day of school, "Oh, you're Reggie's little brother. He was one of the best students I've ever had."

They didn't say, "Let's see if you match up," but that's what Sterling knew they meant.

The thing was, that stuff usually didn't bother Sterling very much. He was a good student himself—maybe even as good as Reggie.

And Sterling was a good athlete. His dad had told him once that for his age, he was a better baseball player than Reggie had been. But when it came to soccer, Sterling was merely good, not great, and Reggie was great at *everything* he did.

When Sterling got home, his mother was there. She had just gotten home from work. She was the manager of a little shop in the mall. She put in long hours.

Sterling's father was an airline pilot. He would leave for two or three days at a time, but then he was home for a few days. So he saw as many of Sterling's games as he could.

That was good sometimes. And lousy sometimes.

Like today.

"How did it go?" Mom wanted to know.

Sterling mumbled, "I blew the game," and he walked by her. He went upstairs to his room, and he lay down on his bed.

"I lost it for us," he told himself. He kept thinking what a big victory it would have been if he hadn't messed up.

The tears came to his eyes again.

When his mom called him down to dinner, he didn't go. He didn't want to hear what he knew his parents and his two sisters would tell him. And he didn't want to sit across the table from Reggie, who would tell him that he shouldn't feel bad.

But his mother understood. She brought him up some dinner, and she said, "I know you feel bad, Sterling. So I told everyone to leave you alone. But I do want you to remember all the games you've won for your teams. Remember that home run you—"

"That was baseball, Mom. I can play *that* game."

That's when Sterling realized that he might quit the soccer team. If he wasn't any good at soccer, maybe he shouldn't try. That idea suddenly made sense.

For the next couple of hours he kept telling himself that he had his answer. He would talk to the coach tomorrow. Then he wouldn't go to practice. When the Pride played the Bandits on Thursday, Sterling just wouldn't be there. All the pressure would be off. He would just take a break from sports for the rest of the fall. People around Angel Park followed the teams, and he would have to answer a lot of questions. But he figured he could live with that.

He was relieved to know what he was going to do. But he wasn't very happy when his mom yelled up the stairs, "Sterling, you have company. They're coming up."

He didn't want to see any of his friends, and most of all he didn't want to see anyone from the soccer team. But that's who came to his door.

It was Jacob and Heidi and Nate.

They were three friends who hung around together a lot. They were Sterling's friends, too.

"Look, you guys, I don't want to hear it, okay?" he told them.

"Hear what?" Jacob said.

But Heidi said, "I don't blame you, Sterling." She walked past Jacob and sat down on Sterling's bed. And then she bounced up and down a couple of times. "I heard it when you stood up. Don't you guys just hate a squeaky mattress. Listen to that. No wonder he doesn't want to hear it."

She bounced a couple more times, but there was no squeak at all. "Wow, that's terrible," she said. "I wonder if you should oil these things."

Suddenly Heidi dropped to her knees and raised up the bedspread. She pushed up the mattress and looked underneath. "Oh, yeah, that's your problem. You need to add some oil."

"Heidi, you're not funny," Sterling said. He leaned against the wall and tucked his fingers into his pockets.

"I've been told that, sir. But you're the guy with a problem, so don't change the subject. Just change your oil."

Nate didn't give Sterling a chance to say anything. He said, "Heidi, that's *not* what Sterling was talking about. Sure his bed squeaks, but he's gotten used to it. What he doesn't want to hear is the sound of wolves at night. It's a lonesome sound, my friend, and it makes a cowboy miss his folks back home."

"No, no, no," Jacob said, and he was acting very serious. "That's not it. What Sterling hates is the sound of all those reptiles out there in the desert. There's nothing worse than waking up to the sound of a barking lizard. Listen, I think I hear one now."

"You're weird, you know it?" Sterling said,

and he was trying not to smile. "All three of you are really weird. Get out of my room before I kick you out."

"This is a cool room," Heidi said. Her tone had changed, and Sterling could tell she meant it. "Have you been to all these countries?"

The room was filled with model airplanes. A lot of them were hanging in the air. The walls were covered with picture posters from all over the world: Paris, the Swiss Alps, a beach in the Bahamas.

"Yup," Sterling said.

"His dad flies airplanes," Jacob said. "He gets free tickets, and the whole family goes. They've been *everywhere*."

"Not really," Sterling said.

Heidi was still gazing around. "I'm glad I haven't been everywhere."

"Why?" Sterling asked.

"Because then there wouldn't be any new places to go."

Sterling shook his head. It wasn't really that funny, but he couldn't help smiling.

"Weird," he said again. "Heidi, you're the weirdest girl I know."

"Thank you," Heidi said politely. "You're rude."

And then Nate said it. "Sterling, you didn't lose the match. And I don't care if you don't want to hear it. It's true. No *one* player causes a loss, *or* a win."

"Yeah, but one player can mess up. And I messed up plenty today."

"Every player messes up in every game," Heidi said. "The ball wouldn't have even gotten to your end of the field if one of our midfielders had cut it off sooner. That's just how soccer is."

Sterling knew all this stuff. But he still didn't want to hear it. And so he said the one thing that would get to the real point. "I'm quitting."

He got what he wanted. All three of his friends were looking at him now—and they looked shocked. No one said a thing.

"I don't want to talk about it," Sterling added. "I already made up my mind."

But Sterling watched Heidi's eyes, and he saw her look toward the doorway. He turned and saw his dad standing there.

"No way, son," Mr. Malone said.

"Dad, I don't have to play if I don't want to," Sterling said, and now he was mad.

"That's true. If the season hadn't started and you had told me that you didn't want to play this year, I'd say fine. But you don't quit in the middle of things. Not a son of mine. And that's final. You're not going to let your teammates down."

Sterling was surprised. Dad was a big man, but he was no boss. He almost never took a stand like this. In fact, he wasn't as strict as his mom about most things.

But Dad could be stubborn, and Sterling could see that this was going to be one of those times.

"Dad, I'm not good at soccer. I'll help the team by quitting."

"If you weren't good, you wouldn't be starting," Nate said. "You're one of the best players we have."

"That's right," Mr. Malone said. "So don't let me hear any more about it."

He turned and walked away.

"Sterling," Jacob said, "I know how you feel. I messed up a lot in baseball. But I also made some plays that helped win games. That's just what happens in sports."

But Jacob didn't really understand. Even Dad didn't know what Sterling was feeling. The other Pride players didn't have big brothers who *never* messed up.

"I gave up that one goal earlier in the match," Nate said. "I came out of the goal too soon, and Klaus passed off. It was a dumb mistake, but I'm not quitting."

Sterling knew he wasn't quitting either. His dad had settled that one. But he still said, "Look, I just don't want to talk about it right now."

And his friends seemed to understand. "Well, we'll see you at practice tomorrow," Nate said. "Just forget about it by then, okay?"

Sterling didn't answer. As the others left

the room, he walked over and lay down on his bed.

"I still say that mattress needs oil," Heidi said as she walked out the door.

Sterling didn't smile this time.

# ★ 4 ★

# Practice

The next day Coach Toscano ran the Pride players through their usual drills—and plenty of them. Then he said he wanted to work on their "transition game." But before he showed them what he meant, he had them sit down on the grass.

"There is something you need to understand about soccer," he told them. "When a team gets its defense back and ready—all set up—the attacking team hardly ever scores. That's why the key to soccer is in those first few seconds after the control of the ball changes from one team to the other."

Coach Toscano was smiling a little, the way he always did. To Sterling, it seemed that he loved to play soccer, to practice, even to talk about it. The idea of a team playing its best was exciting to him.

But Sterling knew something else. The reason he was talking about "transitions" today was that that's where the team had lost the game against the Kickers.

That's where *Sterling* had lost the game.

"The instant our defense takes over the ball, you must become attackers. You must move the ball quickly before the other team can adjust and get back. The team that responds first will win most soccer matches."

Clayton Lindsay held up his hand.

The guy always had something to say. Sterling wished he would just listen, like the rest of the team.

"But if players run upfield quickly right after they take control, and the other team steals the ball back, that's one of the most dangerous times. That's why the fullbacks have to think defense all the time, even when their team is on attack."

Clayton was talking to Sterling, and Sterling knew it. He was describing the exact mistake that Sterling had made in the game against the Kickers.

But Sterling didn't have to be told. He would never make that mistake again. If his dad said he couldn't quit the team, then he wouldn't quit. But he was never going to blow another game by trying to score. He would stay back and play defense, no matter what.

And just because he was going to finish the season didn't mean he had to like soccer. From now on he would be careful not to mess up, and once the season was over, he wouldn't play the game again. He'd stick to baseball and tennis—sports he was better at.

Coach Toscano agreed with Clayton, but then he said, "But no player can think of himself as a defensive player or an attacker. Every fullback is an attacker. And every forward is a defender. Everyone but the goalie must be a potential scorer and potential stopper."

Clayton raised his hand again.

Some of the players groaned.

Jacob was sitting next to Sterling. He turned and said, "Just because he grew up in England, he thinks he knows more than *anyone* about soccer."

Sterling nodded.

Nate was on the other side of Sterling, and he said, "He *does* know a lot."

Sterling knew that was true, but he hated to hear Nate say it. It made him feel that Nate was on Clayton's side.

"Yes, Clayton?" the coach said. He was still smiling.

"Even when fullbacks go on attack, don't they have to keep a defensive position, so they never get caught off guard? That's what our coach in England always said."

"Yes, that's basically true," Coach Toscano answered. "But sometimes, on the best teams, a fullback will see a break and move all the way in for the score. That means a midfielder has to see that and rotate into a defensive position. That's why a team has to work together, make adjustments—and *talk* to each other on the field."

But Sterling knew that most kids didn't play together well enough to do that kind of rotating. *He* was the one who would get blamed if the defense was out of position. It wasn't worth trying.

"Let's try some five-on-five play, and I'll show you what I mean," Coach Toscano told the players. So they all got up, and he showed them what he wanted them to do.

The whole idea was like a fast break in basketball. The instant someone made a steal, the players had to break upfield and get themselves into open space for a pass. The ball had to move rapidly before the defense set up. But the players had to be careful not to get ahead of the ball. Otherwise, they'd get called offsides.

As the team practiced, the players were soon doing a much better job. No one was using the transition as a chance to rest or catch an extra breath. As soon as the defender took the ball from the attacking team, players would yell "Attack!" and everyone would push the ball up the field.

But Sterling held back. He helped the fullbacks get the ball into midfield. Then he hung back and watched the player he was marking on defense. He made sure he was always the player closest to his own goal.

Coach Toscano didn't say anything to him about that, and Sterling felt he was doing the right thing. He was doing a job for the team that someone needed to do. He may not score, but he would keep the other team from scoring.

After practice, however, when all the players were getting on their sweats, Coach Toscano said to Sterling, "Come here just a moment. I want to talk to you."

Sterling walked over to the coach, who was standing away from the other players.

Coach Toscano put his arm around Sterling's shoulder. "Sterling," he said, "have you put that last game out of your mind?"

Sterling knew what the coach wanted him to say, but he couldn't say it. "No," he answered. He wiped the sweat off his forehead with his sleeve. "I'm not going to mess up like that again. Not ever."

"You can't think about *not* making mistakes, Sterling. You have to think about doing something positive."

"I am thinking that. I'm going to play good defense."

"That's fine. But that's not all I'm asking of you. You're fast. You could be a powerful force on our attack. You heard what I said today."

Sterling nodded, as if he agreed, but inside he knew what he planned to do.

The coach seemed to see that Sterling was still doubting himself. "Sterling, you can't keep telling yourself that you lost that last match. You made some—"

"I *did* lose it."

"That's not true." And then the coach told Sterling the same things his friends had told him. Sterling listened, but he remembered what Clayton had said.

And so the coach let him go. He told him to relax and enjoy the game and not to be afraid to attack.

Sterling said he would, but deep down he knew he couldn't do that.

As he walked away from the coach, Jacob and Nate and Heidi were still waiting.

Sterling expected Heidi to tease him, or say something funny, but instead she said, "I hope the coach told you to forget about the last match."

"Yeah," Sterling said, "that's exactly what he told me."

"Have you done it?"

"Sure," Sterling said. But he couldn't look Heidi in the eye.

# Watch for Bandits

Before the match with the Paseo Bandits, all the Angel Park players were saying they *had* to win. If they started the season with two losses, they would never have a chance to win the championship.

Sterling thought that was true. But what he feared even more than losing the match was being the guy who lost it.

When the coach talked to the team, he said, "Players, we played very well when we beat this team in the preseason tournament. Remember how tough our defense was. We shut down Oshima. And that's what we'll have to do again today."

Sterling could tell that the coach was excited. He was having fun. He didn't look worried at all.

"But what we didn't do that last time," the coach continued, "was keep really good pressure on *their* defense. Remember what we practiced this week."

As soon as the coach told the players to do their stretching and get ready to play, Clayton took the chance to look toward Sterling and Jared and say, "Just remember, you fullbacks, if you give Oshima an inch, he'll have you. You just *can't* let him get behind you."

He didn't say, "The way you let Peter Vandegraff get behind you," but Sterling knew what he meant.

And when the kickoff came, that's exactly what Sterling had on his mind. As soon as the Bandits lined up, Sterling saw that they had changed their attack. Oshima had been moved from midfield to forward.

"Sterling," Coach Toscano called, "mark Oshima. Stay on him *tight*."

Sterling made up his mind that he was going to stay on Oshima like a rash. The guy wasn't going to get free for a single second.

But the match had hardly begun before Oshima suddenly dropped back and away from Sterling and took a pass from the girl who played left wing. He turned and dribbled straight at Sterling.

Sterling knew how well Oshima could fake and how quick he was once he made a break. So Sterling didn't gamble. He stayed back a little and kept himself balanced. He told himself to watch the ball and not fall for any body feints.

Oshima saw that Sterling was staying off a little, and so he didn't try to beat him. He passed off to a tall boy named Wadley, another forward.

Oshima walked a few steps, as though he were just waiting around, and then—*bam*—he broke for the goal. But Sterling had never stopped marking him, and he was ready. He broke with Oshima, spotted the pass coming, and stepped up and stole the ball.

Tammy shouted "Attack!" and darted upfield immediately, and Sterling got the ball to her. She dribbled forward, passed off to Clayton, and the Pride had the advantage as they moved quickly up the field.

But Sterling let them go. He stayed back. Oshima had sprinted back to try to help out the defense, so Sterling knew there was no danger from him.

Still, someone might break away, and if that happened, Sterling would be waiting.

The Pride attack bogged down. The Paseo defense recovered. When Chris Baca tried to center the ball to Heidi, a big fullback marked her very close. When she tried to pass off, another Bandit fullback sneaked in for the steal.

Paseo came on the attack, and Sterling was ready. But he had plenty of time. Clayton took on a midfielder and stopped him cold.

For a while the ball changed control several times, and neither team could get very far past the halfway line.

Oshima moved back a little more each time to help the midfielders. Sterling stayed close, but he also allowed enough room so that Oshima wouldn't fake and slip by him. Oshima soon learned that Sterling had the speed to stay with him.

So Oshima kept passing off and then trying to shake Sterling long enough to get a return pass.

But the Bandits' attack depended too much on Oshima. When he couldn't get by Sterling, the other players tried too hard to pass to him anyway. Sterling took advantage over and over again and cut off the passes.

One time when he stole the ball, he dropped it back to Nate, who saw Clayton breaking up the field. Nate took a couple of steps and then punted the ball long to Clayton.

Clayton leaped and controlled the pass with his chest. Then he dropped it straight to his feet. But when he turned to head up-field, he was facing two fullbacks. He quickly passed off to Heidi. She zipped past him and angled off to the left.

One of the Bandit fullbacks marked her. The other stayed with Clayton. But Clayton ran hard and got a step on his defender. Jacob was running upfield at the same time, off to Clayton's left.

Clayton controlled a return pass from Heidi and slammed on the brakes. He lost his man long enough to lead Jacob with a beautiful pass.

Jacob was covered well, but he caught up with the ball and controlled it. And then he seemed to sense what Clayton would do.

Clayton ran toward the corner of the goal, and Jacob stopped suddenly to give himself room. He kicked underneath the ball and lifted a high pass to Clayton.

Clayton leaped like a long jumper and met the ball. But he had no angle to try a header into the net. He headed the ball across the center.

And Heidi was there.

It was beautiful, as though all three players were parts of one smooth machine.

Heidi caught the ball on the inside of her left foot and then took a hard swing with the other leg.

But she only faked the shot. The goalie took the fake and broke to his left, and then Heidi simply nudged the ball behind him.

It rolled into the net.

*Goal!*

The whole team leaped into the air as though they were shocked with the same bolt of electricity. And then everyone ran to Heidi to congratulate her.

Except Sterling. He stayed back.

He cheered and yelled to the other players. But he was too far away to run all the way to Heidi.

And he felt pretty good. He had taken the ball from Oshima and had helped make a quick transition to attack. And all the time the team was driving upfield, he was ready in case someone made a mistake.

As far as Sterling was concerned, he had done his job.

Oshima and the Bandits yelled to each other that they had to get going. They weren't going to lose to Angel Park *again*.

The next time the Bandits got control of the ball, they came hard, and all out. The whole team pressed upfield. Oshima got the ball and seemed to make up his mind to show Sterling who was boss.

He charged at Sterling, stopped cold, faked a pass, and then tried to break past him. Sterling held his ground and his position. He tackled Oshima and stripped the ball loose.

Billy Bacon ran the ball down, and Sterling yelled, "*Attack!*"

He cut past Oshima and took a good pass from Jared. Sterling had room, and he took advantage of his speed. He drove the ball forward, and he stayed a step ahead of Oshima.

When another defender left his mark to cut Sterling off, Sterling saw that Henry

White was all alone. He pushed the ball off the outside of his foot, over to Henry, who made a good run up the right touchline.

For an instant Sterling saw his chance to go with Henry all the way to the goal.

But just as quickly he made a decision to drop off.

He stopped quickly and then faded back to a defensive position.

But Jacob ran past as Sterling slowed. He wasn't in the strong position Sterling had been, but he was fast. He ran toward the goal as Henry moved up the right side.

A defender had a good angle on Henry and held him from moving toward the middle. Henry was forced toward the corner of the field. He slowed, and then he tried to cut inside, past the defender.

But the defender took him on and took control of the ball. Just as quickly, Henry jumped back in and fought for it. He knocked it loose, and the ball bounced directly to Clayton, who had been coming to help.

Clayton instantly spun and crossed a pass to Jacob.

Jacob took the pass with his back to the goal. He dribbled across the front of the goal area and then tried to pass off to Heidi. But a Bandit fullback got a foot on the ball and knocked it away from her.

The ball was rolling across the goal area, and Jacob reacted more quickly than his defender. He darted to the ball and scooped it up with his right foot.

Jacob took a shot, but the defender got back quickly enough to block it. The ball rebounded away from the goal. That's when Clayton's instinct worked again. He was in the perfect spot.

He dropped the ball off his thigh and then drove a powerful shot, low and hard, right between two defenders.

The goalie's vision was blocked, and the ball zipped past him before he had a chance to move.

*WHAM!!!!*

Into the net, and the Pride was up by 2.

Billy had stayed back on defense, and he spun toward Sterling. "Hey, man," he yelled, "we *kill* these guys today!" He slammed Sterling with a high-five. "They're not in the same *league* with us."

Sterling was happy.

But he was also thinking that the team had a long way to go. He wasn't about to forget what had happened in the last match.

# ★ 6 ★

# Staying Tough

At halftime the score was still 2 to 0, and the Pride players were feeling good.

So was Coach Toscano. "Kids," he said, "you're playing great. Even better than last time."

"Sterling is shutting Oshima down," Clayton said. "He's winning the game for us."

Sterling couldn't believe it. He had thought Clayton had it in for him.

The coach agreed with Clayton. "That's right. And that's exactly why I like to have fast fullbacks. Some teams put all their speed up front, and then the fullbacks don't have a chance against the other teams' forwards."

Sterling suddenly felt better than ever.

Maybe defense wasn't so bad, even if he never made any goals.

But then the coach surprised him. "But Sterling made one big mistake in the first half."

That was the last thing Sterling wanted to hear. His heart sank. He couldn't think of a single mistake. Oshima had never once gotten between him and the goal.

"Sterling made a good steal, and a good break upfield," Coach Toscano said. "That was a perfect time to keep on going. When you fullbacks and midfielders see that, someone should fall back and yell out that you're covering. But Sterling wasn't sure you'd do that, so he dropped back."

"But we scored that time," Jacob said.

That was *exactly* what Sterling was thinking.

"Yes. But we got a little lucky. The first break up the field got stopped, but Clayton picked up a blocked shot and kicked it home. If Sterling had kept going, who knows? We might have kept the advantage and gotten a quick goal."

Sterling looked down at the grass. Maybe that was true. But what if he had kept going and someone had lost the ball? And what if no one covered for him at the other end?

"All I'm saying is that you're playing great, Sterling," the coach said. "But you're being a little too careful. You've got to rely on your teammates, and you've got to use your speed at both ends of the field when the chance is there."

"Still, this second half, we have to be careful," Clayton said. "If Sterling moves forward, someone *must* cover for him."

"Sure, we have to cover. But you can't start playing *carefully*. When you do that, you lose your momentum, and the other team puts the pressure on you. What we have to do is keep the pressure on *them*. That's the best defense there is."

Clayton shot a quick glance at Sterling, and Sterling saw his concern. He knew what Clayton was thinking: "Maybe so. But don't mess up by thinking you're a forward all of a sudden."

Sterling got a drink, and he thought things over. One thing was very clear to him. If the Bandits never scored, he didn't have to worry.

The Pride had the lead, and all they had to do was keep it. No matter what the coach said, he was going to stay on Oshima like a shadow. He would let the rest of the team worry about scoring.

When Sterling stepped away from the water fountain, Jacob was waiting for him. "That was true what the coach said. You were way ahead of me that time. You should have become the forward and I could have come with you, and we would have had three-on-one up that right side."

"Yeah," Sterling said. "But if someone had lost the ball and gotten back upfield the other way, everyone—especially Clayton—would want to know what I was doing way up there."

"I don't think so. Clayton would know you had done the right thing, and he would have put the blame where it should be."

Nate had just stepped up to them. "That's right," he said. "Clayton can make you mad, because he says exactly what he thinks. But he knows soccer, and he's fair. He meant what he said about you playing great defense."

Sterling shrugged. He wasn't sure.

"But the coach is right, too. When you get a chance, push the ball up the field. The rest of us just have to yell for a midfielder to drop back."

Sterling didn't say anything. But he was starting to tell himself that maybe that was right. As long as his teammates rotated and covered, he couldn't . . .

But just then Sterling saw his brother. Reggie hadn't made it to the first half. But he was there now, and that changed things. More than ever, Sterling didn't want to do anything stupid.

When the second half started, Sterling was ready for Oshima. But one thing worried him. Some of the substitutes were in the game now. Adam Snarr was in for Lian Jie. He wasn't quite as quick as Lian. That made the Pride weaker in the middle.

What was worse was that Trenton Daynes and Tanya Gardner were both in at fullback positions. Jared and Tammy were better defenders. That meant Sterling felt more on his own on the defensive end of the field.

And the pressure soon became real. Sterling could still make life tough for Oshima, but when Oshima passed off, the other

Bandit forwards were finding more room to move.

About four minutes into the second half, Oshima passed to a kid named Reilly, who had played baseball against Sterling. He was playing right wing.

After Oshima passed off, he dropped away from the goal, and he took Sterling with him.

Reilly hit Wadley, the big forward, with a good pass. Wadley got away from Trenton and charged at Nate.

Nate was in a good position, but Wadley drove a hard shot, low and to Nate's left. Nate dove and got his hands on the ball. But it slipped through his fingers and rolled into the net.

The Bandits had their first goal, and they were excited. Sterling saw their confidence take a huge jump.

Clayton hurried over to Sterling. "Oshima is clearing you out on purpose," Clayton told him. "Switch off, or double, but don't leave the defense up to Trenton and Tanya."

Sterling said okay, but he didn't like the idea of giving Oshima any room at all. He glanced over at his brother. He wondered what Reggie was thinking. What would he think if Sterling dropped off his man and got burned?

The next time the Bandits got close, Oshima tried to pull Sterling away from the goal again. Sterling stayed back and helped Trenton cover Wadley.

Oshima saw what was happening, and he tried to come back for a pass. Clayton had moved in on him, helping out, and Clayton cut off the pass.

As the Pride headed back up the field on attack, Sterling realized what a good move that had been. Clayton really did know his soccer.

Oshima tried the trick one more time, and Sterling stayed back again. That's when Sterling heard the Bandits' coach yell, "Never mind, Kyle. He's not coming with you."

Sterling felt good. As Oshima moved forward, Sterling got on Oshima like glue again.

Trenton was doing better as he got more into the game. And the Pride defense was doing a great job of helping the fullbacks. They were reacting quickly during the transition to defense, and now the Bandits were having trouble.

And then the Bandits, who were starting to get desperate to make the tying goal, were a little too slow on their own switch to defense.

The Bandits made a bad pass, and Tanya cut it off. She saw Sterling make a break, and Nate yelled, "Attack." She made a good lead pass to Sterling, and he was in the open, running hard.

This was his chance.

Maybe.

He saw a midfielder closing in, and he kicked the ball off to Adam, who was running alongside him. Then he cut behind Adam and used him as a screen. Oshima got brushed off, and he was behind again. Sterling took a perfect return pass.

As Sterling crossed the halfway line, he was really rolling. It was a good time to show what he could do.

And yet he wondered. He was taking a big chance.

Sterling passed off to Clayton. He could have kept right on going, but he hesitated and looked back. Oshima was right behind him. When Sterling slowed, Oshima turned on his speed and got between Sterling and the goal.

Sterling's chance to get in on the action was gone.

He held up and then floated back a little. As it turned out, the Bandits regained their strength. The Pride never got off a shot.

As soon as the Bandits took control, Sterling fell back quickly and readied himself for the attack.

But he knew.

If he had kept on pushing, he just might have been in on a goal. And another goal right now would just about bury the Bandits. Now the match was still raging, and the Bandits were going all out to tie it up.

But the Pride defense stayed tough. When some of the starters returned to the field, the Bandits couldn't penetrate at all. The closer the game got to the end, the more defensive-minded the Angel Park players became.

Nate was directing his players, yelling to them where to cover. When the Bandits got deep into Pride territory, the Pride went into their matchup zone. Nothing got through.

Even though Angel Park didn't generate much of a threat of a score themselves, the defense held the Bandits off.

And then, suddenly, the whistle was sounding, and the Pride had its first win.

Billy Bacon jumped on Sterling and yelled, "I told you we'd get these guys. They're *nothing*."

Sterling was glad for the win. He celebrated with his friends. But he wasn't jumping around quite the way most of them were. No matter what Billy was claiming, this had been a tough, close match. And something—Sterling wasn't exactly sure what—was bothering him.

When he walked off the field, his brother hurried toward him. "Hey, great match," Reggie said. "Man, you were all over that forward. He's a good player, but you weren't giving him room to breathe. You're a tough defender, Sterling."

Sterling smiled. He liked that.

Coach Toscano came by, patted Sterling on the shoulder, and said, "Great match." Sterling felt even better.

But the coach started to walk away and

then stopped. "You know, Sterling," he said, "there are different kinds of mistakes you can make in soccer. If a guy beats you and gets a goal, or if you get an open shot and miss, you feel bad. And you feel like everyone saw your mistake."

He paused and smiled. Sterling knew what was coming.

"But what about missed opportunities? When you have a chance to do something positive, that's no time to pull out of the action—just because you're afraid of making a mistake. Think about that."

Coach Toscano had picked a bad time to say something like that. Maybe it was true, but if only he could have waited until Reggie wasn't around.

Reggie picked up on the coach's words. "Yeah, what about that time you had that breakaway with those other guys, and all of a sudden, you just pulled up? That's a time when a fullback with your speed shouldn't be afraid to go to the front."

"I wasn't afraid," Sterling said. "I was just being careful."

But he didn't like his own answer.

# Something Special

When Sterling got home, he told his mom that his team had won, and Reggie told her that Sterling had played a great game. So why didn't he feel any better?

He went up to his room, and sat on his bed. He didn't feel as bad as he had after the last match, but he didn't feel happy either.

When the phone rang, Mrs. Malone yelled upstairs that the call was for Sterling. He walked into his parents' bedroom and picked up the phone there.

He knew the coach's voice immediately.

"Sterling, I was wondering, could you help me with something tomorrow?"

"I guess," Sterling said.

"Okay. It will take a couple of hours. Could I pick you up at four in the afternoon?"

"Sure. But what are we going to do?"

"Well, it's a track meet. They need a few guys to be judges and timers—that sort of stuff."

"Oh. Well, okay." But when Sterling put the phone down, he wondered. He had never heard of a track meet in the fall. The high school had cross-country races, but they were not usually called "track meets."

In fact, all the next day Sterling wondered. The coach had seemed a little mysterious, as though he didn't want to explain. At school, when Sterling asked some of the Pride players what they knew about it, they said the coach hadn't called them.

When the coach picked Sterling up that afternoon, he talked about everything else, but he didn't explain anything more about the track meet. When Sterling saw that they were heading for the high school, he asked, "Is this a high school meet?"

The coach only said, "No. That's just where the meet is being held."

It wasn't until the two walked into the stadium that Sterling realized what was going on. He saw a group of kids in sweats getting off a school bus. He could tell that some were handicapped, and he knew this was some sort of Special Olympics.

Sterling didn't know how he felt about that. Some of the kids looked strange. It seemed unfair to make them run when it wasn't something they could be very good at.

Sterling walked with the coach, but he stayed back a little. He hoped he could get a job timing, maybe, and not have to get too involved.

But a woman was barking, "Escorts over here, please!"

Coach Toscano turned and said, "I told them you'd be an escort. You just take the athletes up to the line and make sure they understand where they have to run—that sort of thing."

"Couldn't I be a timer?" Sterling asked.

"No. I think they have enough. They need escorts."

So Sterling followed the woman. But he felt really strange. He didn't know how to talk to kids like the ones he was seeing all around him.

When he got his first assigned athlete, he was really nervous. The guy was bigger than Sterling, and older. He had a large head, and he smiled all the time. Sometimes he hung his head to the side. Saliva ran from his mouth.

"This is James," the woman told Sterling. "He's going to run the hundred-meter dash. Take him down to the starting line." She pointed to the other end of the field. "What is your name?"

"Sterling."

"James, this is Sterling," she said. "He's going to show you where you'll run. Okay?"

"Okay," the big boy said, slowly, and then he laughed.

"Come down this way," Sterling said.

"Take him by the arm and show him," the woman said.

So Sterling took James by the arm, and the two walked away together. "I'm gonna run," James said.

"Can you run fast?" Sterling asked, trying to think of something to say.

"Yes. Very fast." He laughed again.

But James couldn't even walk all that well. He shuffled his feet slowly, and he gazed off into the air. At times he seemed to forget in which direction they were heading.

"Do you like to run?" Sterling asked.

"Yes," James said.

"Do you think you can win?"

"Yes."

Sterling felt sorry for James. He seemed nice—some of Sterling's nervousness was now gone—but the poor guy would take forever to run a hundred meters. Why did anyone want to put him through that? It almost seemed a way of making fun of him.

"Run *fast*," James said. When he laughed, he sort of gurgled.

When the two boys finally reached the starting line, other escorts and other racers were arriving. A young man in a T-shirt stepped over to Sterling and said, "James gets a little mixed up about where to run. You might have to walk along with him and make sure he gets to the finish line."

"Do you think maybe he's a little too . . . you know . . ."

The young man laughed. "James is great," he said. "This is your first time at a meet like this, isn't it?"

Sterling nodded. He felt bad. Some of the kids didn't look handicapped. A couple of boys were even doing stretching exercises. He could tell that they would beat James by a mile. He couldn't figure out why people would organize a meet like this and not give a boy like James a fair chance.

But James kept saying, "Run *fast*."

"That's right," Sterling told him. "I'll help

you. I think you can beat some of these guys."

James laughed and said, *"Yeah!"*

Sterling made up his mind that he was going to help James beat at least one of the racers. He didn't want the poor guy to come in dead last.

But it wasn't going to be easy. Some of the guys took their sweats off, but James didn't want to. And when everyone lined up at the starting line, James hardly paid any attention.

"Come on, James, get ready," Sterling told him.

When the gun fired, everyone started out rather slowly, but James didn't start at all. Sterling jumped out in front of him, grabbed his arm, and pulled him. "Come on. Come on."

But the starter said, "Don't pull him. Let him run his own race. Just guide him if you have to."

Sterling let go, but he screamed, *"Come on, James! Come on!"*

And James began his run. It was only a little faster than his walk. It was a shuffle step, slow and awkward, and most of the runners were long gone.

Sterling still thought James had a chance to catch one of the other racers if he would try a little harder. But James didn't seem to pay much attention to that.

*"Come on,* James! Come on. You can catch that guy!" Sterling kept yelling.

James was smiling, and he kept moving at the same pace. It didn't take Sterling long to realize that James was going to be last, no matter what. And so Sterling quit yelling and just walked along close to James.

And he watched the smile that never left James's face. "Run *fast,"* he said every few steps. "Run *fast."*

James still hadn't made fifty meters when all the others were finished, but Sterling had forgotten all that now. He just kept watching James's face. The big smile. The joy.

On and on James kept shuffling. "Run *fast,"* he said again and again. By now

Sterling saw something in James that he didn't really understand.

What he did know, however, was that he liked James.

When James finally got to the finish line, a girl ran up to him and put her arms around him. "Good run," she said. "Way to go."

"His name is James," Sterling said.

"Way to go, James," the girl said, and she stepped back and put a ribbon around his neck.

"Run *fast*," James said.

"That's right," Sterling said. "Way to go, James. You ran fast!"

James looked down at the medal hanging from the ribbon. He gripped it awkwardly and held it up for Sterling to see.

"You won it, James," Sterling said. "That's your medal."

"I won," James said, and he laughed.

James was only the first of many athletes Sterling met. Some of the runners he escorted were pretty fast, and some could talk more clearly. But all of them were happy when they finished their races, and everyone got a medal. Everyone seemed satisfied with what they had done.

Sterling hardly knew how to explain to himself what he was feeling. But he kept going back to find James, and each time he did, James was overjoyed.

It wasn't until Sterling was back in the car with his coach that he even tried to express what he had experienced. "Those kids all did their best, didn't they?" he said.

Coach Toscano said, "Yes, they did. And they all won."

"Did you bring me here for some reason, Coach?"

"Yes, I did."

"What was it?"

"Well, I'll let you think about it."

So the coach dropped Sterling off at his house, and Sterling went up to his room. And he did think.

It was strange that James didn't have to beat anyone, yet he really had won.

Sterling, on the other hand, kept racing his own brother—who wasn't even on the track—and he never won.

# ★ 8 ★

# Tornado Warning

The Angel Park team had a bye for Monday's game, so that meant they had a whole week to practice before they took on the Santa Rita Tornadoes the next Thursday.

Santa Rita had beaten the Pride during preseason, so the players knew that this was going to be a big match. Angel Park had to beat one of the best teams in the league to prove to themselves that they were going to compete for the championship.

Or at least that's what the Angel Park players were saying.

Sterling wanted to win, but he felt different about things. At practice each day he worked harder than he ever had before. He knew he had to be a better dribbler and shooter if he wanted to be a complete player.

"Run *fast*," Sterling kept saying to himself. He had his own idea what that meant, even though he never tried to put it into words. But one thing it did mean was, "Just do your best."

By the time the week had passed and the time for the match had come, Sterling could feel his improvement. He was anxious to play and have fun.

When he saw his mom and dad and Reggie walking toward the field, he looked away and said, "Run *fast*." He didn't want to think his usual thoughts.

But he heard Reggie yell, "Hey, Sterling, you gotta be tough today." Reggie knew what a tough team the Tornadoes were, and now Sterling thought about that.

Some of Sterling's old feelings came back. The thought of messing up in front of Reggie crossed his mind. He thought of that first match, even though he tried not to.

Hugh Roberts, the Tornadoes' mouthy

forward, was already smarting off, even before the kickoff. "How bad did we beat these guys last time?" he yelled to one of his friends.

A lanky kid named "Rocket" Rockwell, the Tornadoes' little ball of speed who had been the catcher on the Santa Rita baseball team, yelled back, "I think it was only about 4 to 2. But we put in all our subs after we knew we had it won."

"You're nuts," Billy Bacon yelled from the sidelines. "We had a bad day. Today, you *die.*"

"Bacon, you *talk* big, but you can't *play* this game," Roberts shouted. "You're as round as you are tall."

Rockwell laughed, but Billy didn't answer. He saw the coach looking at him. But he turned to Sterling and said, "I've got fungus growing between my toes that I like better than those two guys."

Sterling felt about the same. He knew them all too well from baseball, and he was sick of their mouths. He didn't want to lose to them.

So by the time the kickoff came, Sterling was nervous again, same as usual. He just wanted to beat these guys, and he wanted his family to see him do a good job.

As usual, he was marking the toughest forward, and that meant Roberts. Roberts wasn't as fast as Sterling, but he was very experienced. He had all kinds of fakes and moves. When Sterling heard Roberts smarting off, he wanted to do more than stay with the guy. He wanted to strip the guy clean—and shut him up.

"Run *fast*," he told himself. But it wasn't so easy to think that way now.

The early going was even, with both teams having trouble moving the ball against the other's defense. But a couple of minutes into the match, Roberts sprinted to midfield and took a pass from the wing.

He controlled the ball and pivoted so he was facing Sterling.

As Roberts dribbled forward, Sterling gave him room. But he had a surprise in mind. He kept back-pedaling, making Roberts think that he wasn't going to take him on.

And then, suddenly, he closed quickly on Roberts and tried a tackle.

But Roberts was smart. He saw what was coming, and he flicked the ball from his right foot to his left. As Sterling stabbed with his right foot, he missed the ball and ended up off-balance. Roberts slipped past Sterling, and was *gone*.

He had a breakaway, straight at the goal.

Jared saw what was happening and left his man to pick up Roberts.

Roberts kept charging straight ahead, but as Jared closed in on him, he faked a pass to the other forward—Jared's man. Jared took the fake and tried to get back to his own man.

Nate came out of the goal and faced Roberts. But Roberts drove a shot right past him and into the net.

The Tornadoes went crazy.

"This is going to be easy today!" Roberts was yelling. And then he looked at Sterling. "Hey, Malone, if I were you, I'd stick with baseball. You don't play this game too well."

Sterling turned and walked away. He didn't look at his brother or parents. He didn't look at his coach. He just made up his mind not to get beat again.

From that time on, Sterling was unbeatable on defense. He stayed away from the fancy stuff. He didn't try to steal. But he covered Roberts tight no matter where he went.

With Roberts under control, the Tornadoes couldn't get much of a threat going. But then, neither could Angel Park. The match turned into a defensive battle, with neither team getting off many shots.

Gradually the half was coming to a close, and the score was still 1 to 0. Roberts was getting *very* tired of having Sterling all over him, and he didn't mind showing it.

A couple of times, when the referee wasn't looking, Roberts threw an elbow at Sterling, or he tried to trip him.

"You think you're some hot defender," he told Sterling. "But I beat you once already, and I'll beat you again."

Sterling didn't say a word. He just stayed

with Roberts—step for step wherever he ran.

And finally something paid off for the Pride. Clayton and Lian were winning the battle in the middle. They were keeping a lot of pressure on the Santa Rita defense.

But it was a tough defense, and Angel Park had had very few decent shots. The goalie had made a great stop on a shot by Heidi, and that was as close as the Pride had come to scoring.

Just when it appeared Angel Park wouldn't score in the first half, Jacob got a break. Clayton shot him a pass, and the defender, trying to catch up with Jacob, slipped and fell.

He was up quickly, but Jacob had a good lead. He took the ball across the front of the goal area, and he took advantage of being free for the moment.

Jacob smashed a hard, low shot at the left side of the goal, and it would have gotten past the goalie, but a fullback managed to kick out at the ball and deflect it.

The ball bounced off to the left of the goal, and Henry White made a dash for it. He was marked closely, but he got to the ball first, and he flipped it high in front of the net.

It was a perfect center pass.

And Clayton had guessed right.

He charged the goal and leaped above the defenders. He drove the ball with his forehead—down and to the left.

The goalie had seen it coming. He made a good dive, but the ball flew by his outreached hands and into the net.

*All tied up!*

1 to 1.

Sterling felt a lot better. At least his mistake hadn't lost the game. Not yet. And if the Pride could get things going now, maybe they could beat these guys.

Halftime came with the score still tied, and Sterling was glad for the rest.

But he wasn't glad about what the coach told him. "Sterling, good defense. You're making life tough for Roberts." But then the coach added, "When we go back out, I want Trenton to go in for you for a little while."

Coach Toscano told Trenton that he had to stay right on Roberts, the same as Sterling had been doing.

Sterling rarely left the field. He couldn't think why the coach would take him out in a match that was this tight.

Heidi walked over to him and said, "You've got Roberts really shaken. He's screaming for the ball all the time, but no one can get it to him."

"Yeah," Sterling said, "but I wasn't on him tight when he made that goal."

"Don't feel bad about that. He's one of the highest scorers in the league. He's gotten by a lot of people."

Sterling nodded. For a moment that really made sense to him. Why did he have to get so down on himself? He had done his best.

But just then Reggie walked up. "Way to play defense," he said, but he didn't really sound all that pleased. Sterling figured that his brother wanted to see him do more than "play defense."

Sterling thanked Reggie, but then he said, "The coach is putting Trenton in for me."

Reggie looked surprised. "Why?"

"Everyone gets to play."

"I know. But they need you. Can't they take someone else out?"

Sterling shrugged. "I'm the one that gave up the only goal they have," he said.

But Reggie grabbed Sterling by the shoulders. "Hey, look at me," he said. "You *stopped* that team. You shut down their best player. Don't talk to me about messing up. Remember all the good stuff you did."

Sterling was a little surprised that Reggie would say that. He always imagined Reggie standing on the sidelines thinking how bad he was.

"You gotta believe in yourself, Sterling," Reggie said. "And have *fun.* That's why you play. You're too hard on yourself. I mess up, but I don't worry about it. I just get back in there and keep trying."

Sterling had never heard Reggie say anything like that. In Sterling's mind, Reggie never made a mistake.

"Okay," Sterling said. And for the first time in a long time he felt as though Reggie were on his side.

# ★ 9 ★

# Pride Power

When the players went back to the field, Sterling could feel the intensity on both sides. The fans were upping the pressure. "Come on Santa Rita," one big guy kept bellowing, "these kids aren't any good. Put 'em away now."

Sterling wanted to be out there. It was hard to stand on the side and watch.

But the coach called Sterling over and told him, "Trenton doesn't have your speed. He'll do okay for a while, but when he starts tiring, I'll put you back in."

That sounded fair.

As the second half got going, Sterling saw that Trenton was doing a good job. He was in Roberts's face every second, and Roberts really didn't like it.

Roberts was talking more all the time now, and he was doing anything he could to try to shake Trenton. He even knocked him down once. Sterling could tell he had done it on purpose.

"Are you watching Roberts?" the coach asked.

"Yeah," Sterling answered.

"Good. Watch him close."

Sterling thought maybe the coach wanted him to see his moves. But Sterling had seen those moves up close. He knew what it took to stay with the guy.

The only trouble was, not much was happening for either attack right now. Clayton was so powerful in the middle that he could often shut down the Tornadoes' midfield game by himself. And he moved the ball well when he took control.

But the Tornadoes' fullbacks were like Sterling—fast and smart. And they were making life miserable for Heidi and Jacob.

Clayton kept powering his way toward the goal area. He even got off a shot himself.

But he was well covered, and he had a bad angle. The shot went wide of the goal.

The minutes were ticking by, and nothing was happening.

But Trenton was tough on defense. And finally Roberts had all he wanted of that. He watched, and while the referee wasn't looking his way, he slammed Trenton in the back with his forearm.

Trenton crashed on his face. And he was a little slow getting up.

"Did you see that?" Coach Toscano yelled to Sterling.

"Yeah. Tell the ref. He can't do that."

But Sterling knew that the referee couldn't call what he hadn't seen.

Sterling was furious.

But Trenton seemed all right, and he got back on Roberts and stayed on him. Roberts's face was red, and he kept yelling at Trenton. But Trenton ignored all that and just stayed tough.

"So what do you think?" the coach said.

"Think about what?"

"About Roberts."

"I think he's a jerk."

"Maybe." The coach hesitated, as though he wanted Sterling to see something more than that. "Do you think he's having fun?" he asked.

Sterling was surprised by the question. He took another look at Roberts. "No," he said. "He looks like he's mad enough to kill someone."

"So why do we play sports, Sterling?"

"What?"

"Why do we even have sports? What's the point of being out here? Have you been having fun this season?"

Sterling thought about that.

Before Sterling could answer, Coach Toscano asked, "What was that boy's name at the track meet?"

"Who? James?"

"Yeah. Think about James."

Sterling nodded. "What about him?"

"Just remember the way he looked when he won his race. And then look at Roberts out there. Do you see what I'm telling you?"

"Yeah, I do."

"Okay," Coach Toscano said. "Next time we get a break in the action, go back in for Trenton. And Sterling . . ."

"Yeah?"

"Have some fun."

"Okay."

When Sterling went back on the field, he ran out to Roberts and said, "Hey, I'm back. Have you missed me?"

Then he laughed.

Roberts didn't like that. He told Sterling, "Yeah. Because I can beat you any time I want to. So get ready."

For a couple of minutes Sterling was so tight on Roberts that the guy never got control of the ball.

But then Roberts made a hard move upfield, stopped, and dropped back. He got a little daylight between him and Sterling that way, and a midfielder knocked a quick pass to him.

Sterling saw Roberts turn toward him. He caught a quick look at his angry face. He knew that the guy had made up his mind to take the ball to the goal himself. He was going to beat Sterling no matter what it took.

Sterling smiled without meaning to. And he waited, staying back a little.

As Roberts pushed the ball forward, Sterling cut the distance between them, but he didn't try any tackles. He knew that Roberts was going to try to make something happen, and that could mean a mistake.

And then it happened. Roberts liked to cut the ball behind his left foot and then break around a defender on the left side.

Sterling knew the move, and something in Roberts's body angle tipped him off that it was coming. Just as Roberts made his fake to the right, Sterling stayed a little to the left—exactly where he knew the ball was going to be.

When Roberts tried the cut, Sterling was ready, and he kicked the ball loose. It rolled behind Roberts just as he tried to go by Sterling.

Sterling chased the ball down and took it in stride. He burst up the field with the slower Roberts behind him.

Clayton yelled for the ball and broke toward the middle of the field. Sterling hit him with the pass, and then he kept right on running with Clayton.

Sterling heard Lian yell, "I'll drop back."

Sterling was with Clayton, off to his left. When the defense closed in, Clayton kicked the ball back to him.

But Sterling saw Chris Baca open on the left wing, and he passed off quickly.

The Pride was coming hard, but the Tornadoes' fullbacks were packed in and ready. Chris took the ball down the left touchline and then stopped and slipped his man.

But as he broke toward the center of the field, another defender picked him up. Chris passed back to Sterling, but another fullback marked him.

Sterling had been practicing some cuts of his own, and now seemed the time to try something. As he came toward the defender, he knocked the ball from one foot to the other. The defender was marking fairly close but giving ground.

Suddenly Sterling struck the ball harder, to his left and past the fullback. Then he *exploded* toward the ball.

The fullback had been caught with his balance to his left, and Sterling got a step on him. But the goal was still well covered.

That's when Sterling saw Clayton breaking in behind him, and he dropped a pass straight back.

Clayton was coming hard. He took the pass and cut close to Sterling, scraping off his defender. He kept charging and seemed about to shoot.

Two fullbacks converged on him, and the goalie broke to the left side of the net.

Just then Clayton flicked the ball to his right, and sure enough, Sterling had made his move toward the goal. He hardly had to kick the ball to roll it into the right side of the net.

It all seemed so easy—and natural.

Suddenly everyone on the team was mobbing Sterling and screaming, "Great shot! Way to play!"

*2 to 1!*

And that was it for the Tornadoes. They seemed to get more frustrated and Roberts ended up getting a yellow warning card for intentional tripping.

The Pride didn't score again, but they played defense like a swarm of bees. There seemed to be two Pride defenders for every Tornado attacker no matter where the ball was.

And everyone was having fun.

When it was all over, the players congratulated Sterling again. And he knew they meant it. He had scored the winning goal.

But he knew something else about the match. And so did Coach Toscano.

Maybe Reggie had some idea about it too. Reggie asked Sterling, "Did you know that when you came back in the game, you were smiling, and you smiled the whole rest of the time?"

Sterling didn't know that. But he smiled now.

"No kidding. When you made that goal, you were smiling before you stole the ball— and all the way down the field. It was like you knew you were going to score before it happened."

"No, I didn't know that," Sterling said. "I was just having fun."

"You keep it up, and you're even going to be as good as *me!*" Reggie said.

But Sterling looked over at his coach and said, "I just want to run fast—like James."

Heidi and Nate were standing nearby. They both looked surprised. They didn't know who James was. But Coach Toscano gave Sterling a big high-five, and he said, "Now you're talking, Sterling."

Everyone on the team was excited. The Pride was 2 and 1 now, and they had beaten two good teams. If they kept this up, they could go all the way.

"Hey, Sterling," Heidi yelled, "that was some move you made. The coach is going to make a forward out of you."

But Sterling said, "No thanks. I'm a fullback." And he suddenly liked the idea of playing *his* position and not Reggie's.

## League Standings After Four Games:

| | |
|---|---|
| Kickers | 3-0 |
| Springers | 2-1 |
| Pride | 2-1 |
| Tornadoes | 2-2 |
| Gila Monsters | 1-2 |
| Racers | 1-3 |
| Bandits | 1-3 |

### First Match Scores:

| | | | |
|---|---|---|---|
| Kickers | 4 | Pride | 3 |
| Bandits | 5 | Gila Monsters | 2 |
| Tornadoes | 4 | Racers | 2 |
| Springers bye | | | |

### Second Match Scores:

| | | | |
|---|---|---|---|
| Pride | 2 | Bandits | 1 |
| Gila Monsters | 3 | Racers | 2 |
| Springers | 6 | Tornadoes | 3 |
| Kickers bye | | | |

### Third Match Scores:

| | | | |
|---|---|---|---|
| Tornadoes | 2 | Bandits | 0 |
| Kickers | 5 | Racers | 1 |
| Springers | 7 | Gila Monsters | 1 |
| Pride bye | | | |

### Fourth Match Scores:

| | | | |
|---|---|---|---|
| Pride | 2 | Tornadoes | 1 |
| Racers | 3 | Bandits | 2 |
| Kickers | 4 | Springers | 3 |
| Gila Monsters bye | | | |

# Angel Park Soccer Strategies

Soccer, like football and basketball, is a game of game plans, of strategies. Both professionals and amateurs use strategies to give themselves a general sense of what to do *as a team*. Without teamwork and strategy, soccer games would only be a bunch of people running around a field, kicking a ball back and forth.

This is why players have particular jobs to do, either scoring goals or defending against goals. This makes the game more interesting— and more challenging. When a player is running upfield with the ball, he will almost always be cut off before he scores a goal himself. This is why players learn strategies. When the time comes, they'll know what to do. They'll know where their teammates are without even looking.

Or at least that's the idea. The success of the strategies depends on the skill of the players. The strategies we've presented here, in these diagrams, are standard game plans that the Angel Park Pride might attempt to use in a game. If you think your team could profit from a little strategic thinking, show these to your coach. Give them a try. Good luck!

# Kickoff

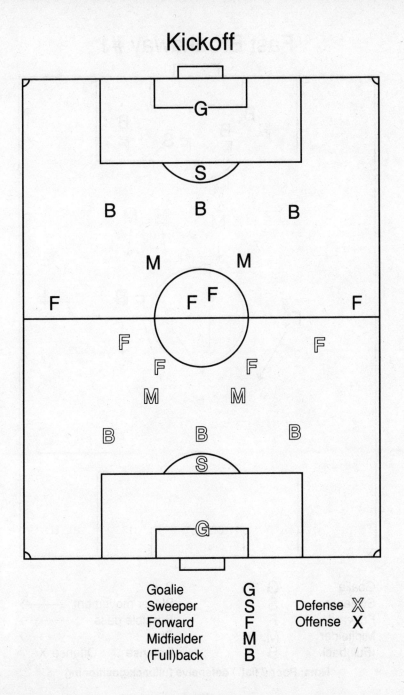

| Goalie | **G** | |
| Sweeper | **S** | Defense 𝕏 |
| Forward | **F** | Offense **X** |
| Midfielder | **M** | |
| (Full)back | **B** | |

# Fast Breakaway #1

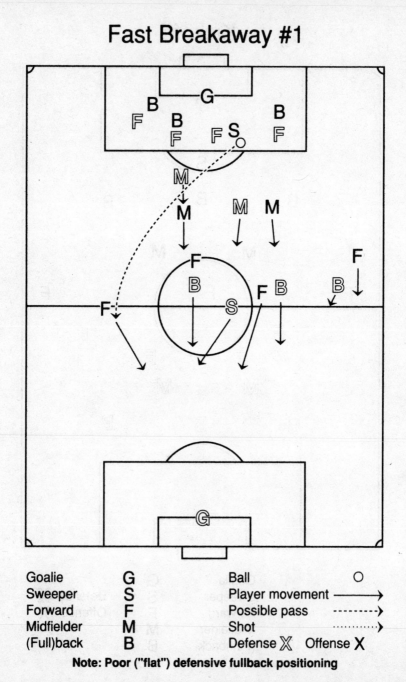

| | | |
|---|---|---|
| Goalie | **G** | Ball ○ |
| Sweeper | **S** | Player movement ——→ |
| Forward | **F** | Possible pass -----→ |
| Midfielder | **M** | Shot ·······→ |
| (Full)back | **B** | Defense X   Offense X |

**Note: Poor ("flat") defensive fullback positioning**

# Fast Breakaway #2

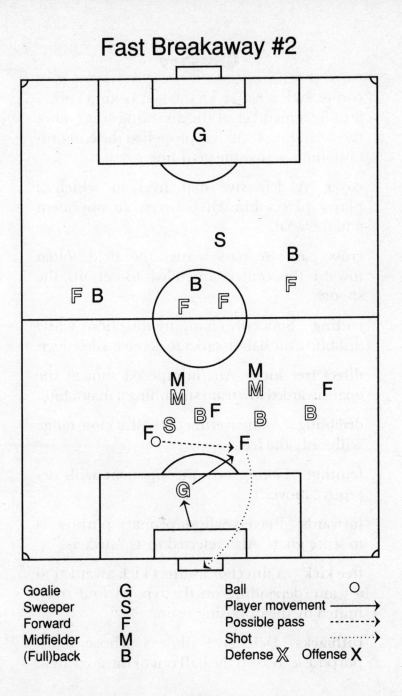

| | | |
|---|---|---|
| Goalie | **G** | Ball ○ |
| Sweeper | **S** | Player movement ——→ |
| Forward | **F** | Possible pass ------→ |
| Midfielder | **M** | Shot ········→ |
| (Full)back | **B** | Defense 𝕏  Offense X |

# Glossary

**corner kick**   A free kick taken from a corner area by a member of the attacking team, after the defending team has propelled the ball out-of-bounds across the goal line.

**cover**   A defensive maneuver in which a player places himself between an opponent and the goal.

**cross pass**   A pass across the field, often toward the center, intended to set up the shooter.

**cutting**   Suddenly changing directions while dribbling the ball in order to deceive a defender.

**direct free kick**   An unimpeded shot at the goal, awarded to a team sustaining a major foul.

**dribbling**   Maneuvering the ball at close range with only the feet.

**feinting**   Faking out an opponent with deceptive moves.

**forwards**   Players whose primary purpose is to score goals. Also referred to as "strikers."

**free kick**   A direct *or* indirect kick awarded to a team, depending on the type of foul committed by the opposing team.

**fullbacks**   Defensive players whose main purpose is to keep the ball out of the goal area.

**goalkeeper**   The ultimate defender against attacks on the goal, and the only player allowed to use his hands.

**halfbacks**   See Midfielders.

**heading**   Propelling the ball with the head, especially the forehead.

**indirect free kick**   A shot at the goal involving at least two players, awarded to a team sustaining a minor foul.

**juggling**   A drill using the thighs, feet, ankles, or head to keep the ball in the air continuously.

**kickoff**   A center place kick which starts the action at the beginning of both the first and second halves or after a goal has been scored.

**marking**   Guarding a particular opponent.

**midfielders**   Players whose main purpose is to get the ball from the defensive players to the forwards. Also called "halfbacks."

**penalty kick**   A direct free kick awarded to a member of the attacking team from a spot 12 yards in front of the goal. All other players must stay outside the penalty area except for the goalie, who must remain stationary until the ball is in play.

**punt**    A drop kick made by the goalkeeper.

**shooting**    Making an attempt to score a goal.

**strikers**    See Forwards.

**sweeper**    The last player, besides the goal-keeper, to defend the goal against attack.

**tackling**    Stealing the ball from an opponent by using the feet or a shoulder charge.

**total soccer**    A system by which players are constantly shifting positions as the team shifts from offense to defense. Also called "position-less soccer."

**volley kick**    A kick made while the ball is still in the air.

**wall**    A defensive barrier of players who stand in front of the goal area to aid the goalkeeper against free kicks.

**wall pass**    This play involves a short pass from one teammate to another, followed by a return pass to the first player as he runs past the defender. Also called the "give-and-go."

**wingbacks**    Outside fullbacks.

**wingers**    Outside forwards.